# The Reading Pig
# Goes to the Desert

**Author**—Jessica Jankowski-Gallo

with Judy Nostrant

**Illustrator**—Judy Nostrant

Teachers
Change Brains
media

Dedicated to
Emily Meschter

Teachers Change Brains Media books may be purchased for educational, business or sales promotional use.
For information – www.thereadingpig.com
Library of Congress Cataloging in Publication Data is available on request.

ISBN – 9780996389150 First edition. July 2018

Book management & marketing services – www.maxfemurmedia.com

Illustrations – Judy Nostrant

Cover layout & pre-press production — Pattie Copenhaver

# Acknowledgements –

The Reading Pig's adventures continue, driven by the contributions of the following students, partners and generous donors.

Emily Meschter, DHL – In 2012, Emily Meschter was awarded an Honorary Doctor of Humane Letters degree by the University of Arizona, College of Education for her long and distinguished career as a philanthropist and supporter of education. In 2010, the Flowing Wells Unified School District honored Emily for her incredible contributions to the district by creating the Emily Meschter Early Learning Center. Emily's support of the "Reading Pig Goes to The Desert" is another example of her extraordinary service to education.

Ms. Jessica's Students – Amerie, Hope, Aliya, Noah, Nolan, Rustin, Makenzie, Liliana, Dylan, Jack, Cora, Bailey, Tatum, Wren, Gabe, Aliana, Mia, Ella, and Benjamin. The Reading Pig salutes you for your creativity and passion for reading and writing. You are published authors!

Judy Nostrant, Illustrator. Judy continues to amaze and delight by capturing the spirit of reading in her illustrations.

Pattie Copenhaver, Graphic Designer. Pattie brings the entire book to life with a very special level of creativity and personal touch.

Tim Derrig, Book Manager. Tim handles all the details, big, small and everything in-between. His passion for this project is larger than life.

Dr. Susan Shinn, Emily Meschter Early Learning Center Director. Dr. Shinn's excitement and relentless desire for her teacher and students to become authors helped make the dream a reality.

Northern Arizona University – As a university partner, NAU continues to support children's literacy through The Reading Pig series.

Pima Federal Credit Union & Simply Bits – A generous grant from PFCU brought The Reading Pig to life in 2016. Simply Bits brought The Reading Pig to life (as they know how) with their creation and development of www.thereadingpig.com

We are grateful for your collective efforts and support,

Nic aka "Dr. C"

© 2018   Nicholas I. Clement
ISBN: 9780996389150
Published by:
Teachers Change Brains Media

www.legendaryteacher.com

# The Reading Pig Goes to the Desert

In 2015, when I recommended Ms. Jessica Jankowski-Gallo for hire at the Emily Meschter Early Learning Center in the Flowing Wells School District, I knew she was special. She has surpassed my highest expectations.

Ms. Jessica's enthusiasm for young children is evident in her planning, instruction and interactions with young children. She views each child as a unique individual and then nurtures that individuality.

After reading aloud Dr. Nicholas Clement's book, *The Reading Pig Goes to School*, Ms. Jessica sat down with her class and discussed the story in detail. During this discussion, Ms. Jessica asked the students where they thought the Reading Pig should go next in this big world. After much deliberation and discussion about the culture and environment where they live, the students decided that the Reading Pig should go to the desert. Ms. Jessica encouraged her students to expand their thoughts and ideas in order to develop a story. As the days passed, the young learners' excitement turned blank pages into words, and the words into a story. The story of the *Reading Pig Goes to the Desert* was born!

*The Reading Pig Goes to the Desert* is written from the hearts and joyfulness of young children. Ms. Jessica skillfully transformed her students' feelings into a manuscript that embraces individuality and expresses the excitement for learning. Ms. Jessica is a Legendary Teacher!

Susan Shinn, Ed. D.

*Enjoy the tale...*

Hi, my name is Cole.

One of my favorite field trips ever was when our preschool class went to the Desert Wildlife Center! We saw all kinds of amazing animals and plants on our desert trip.

It was awesome!

Our teacher Ms. Jessica invited our school Superintendent Dr. C to join us. Dr. C is funny and always brings his pal the Reading Pig.

We got ready for our trip. The desert is hot and dry and we had to wear hats and carry plenty of water.

Dr. C put on his big straw hat and picked up the Reading Pig. Makenzie, Aliana, Liliana, Rustin, Amanda, Wren, Ben, Dr. C, the Reading Pig and I followed Ms. Jessica out to the bus.

The bus was huge!

We had to walk up 3 big steps to get on!

The bus driver greeted us with a smile and told us we could sit anywhere we wanted. Ms. Jessica helped us find seats. We buckled our seat belts and were off! The ride was long and bumpy but lots of fun. Dr. C let each of us hold the Reading Pig!

We sang songs with Dr. C and Ms. Jessica. By the time we were done singing "The Wheels on the Bus", we could see the entrance to the Desert Wildlife Center. We couldn't wait to get off the bus and start exploring!

Ms. Jessica led us off the bus. We gathered around while Dr. C and Ms. Jessica told us some rules to follow at the Desert Wildlife Center.

**1.** Always stay on the trail and stay with the group at all times.

**2.** Don't touch or brush against the cactus! They have sharp spines!

**3.** Always listen to Dr. C and Ms. Jessica.

**4.** Don't touch or feed any of the animals.

We listened carefully and started out on the trail.

The first thing we saw was a giant cactus called a **saguaro**. Ms. Jessica said that it was almost forty feet tall and over 100 years old! It was full of spines and looked like it was waving its arms. My friend Amanda saw a bird peeking out of a hole in the **saguaro,** and Ben pointed to another bird way up high in the cactus.

Dr. C told us some desert birds like to make their homes inside the big cactus. They are very safe in their nests up in the **saguaro**.

The bird Amanda saw peeking out of the **saguaro** is a **Gila woodpecker**.

And the bird Ben spotted is called a **western screech owl**.

Right next to the big saguaro was a **prickly pear cactus**. It had very big and very sharp spines! A little bird was busy munching on its bright red fruit.

"That's a **cactus wren**," said Dr. C.
"He loves the prickly pear fruit!"

People like to eat prickly pear fruit too. You can make really tasty jelly and juice with the red fruit!

Just ahead of us on the trail was a family of birds with little feathers sticking straight up on top of their heads. We learned they are called **Gambel's quail**. The mama, papa and babies were cooling off at a small pool of water.

There were lots of baby **quail.** How many can you find?

We saw some cactus with big bites taken out of them. Two funny looking hairy pigs were busy munching on the cactus. Ms. Jessica said the mama and baby were an animal called a **javelina.** They aren't really pigs, but an animal called a peccary or **javelina.**

The baby **javelina** looked up and saw the Reading Pig. He kept looking at the Reading Pig. I wonder what the little **javelina** was thinking?

The **prairie dog** village was our next stop. We saw a fat **prairie dog** pop up out of his burrow. Then we saw another and another and another! I wondered how many **prairie dogs** were living underground?

**Prairie dogs** live underground in a series of burrows, tunnels and entrances.

The family burrows have sleeping rooms, nurseries, and even toilet areas!

We said goodbye to the **prairie dogs** and got back on the trail. Just then a funny looking bird raced past us.

It was a **roadrunner**! They can actually run faster than people!

The **roadrunner** ran ahead to where the **bighorn sheep** live. Dr. C pointed to the mama **ewe** and her baby **lamb** high up on a rocky ledge. The papa **ram** watched as the lamb climbed on the rocky ledges. I wondered how the little lamb could climb so well. Ms. Jessica told us that **bighorn sheep** are like mountain climbers and are very sure footed.

The papa **bighorn sheep** has huge horns. I guess that's how he got his name.

Next we went to see the **mountain lion**! He walked over and sat down next to the window in his habitat. Ms. Jessica told us the **mountain lion** would stay on his side of the glass window and we were very safe. He was really big and had giant paws! He was the biggest cat I had ever seen!

**Mountain lions** are also known as cougars, pumas or panthers.

We were all a bit tired and hungry. We found a shady spot and sat down for lunch. While we were eating, Dr. C and the Reading Pig brought out a card game.

We took turns matching the words with the pictures. Soon it was time to head back to the bus.

We started back on the trail. Dr. C was at the head of the line, but he wasn't holding the Reading Pig. Ms. Jessica wasn't holding him either. It took us a while to get back to the bus and we still hadn't seen the ReadingPig.

**Where was the Reading Pig?**

We asked Dr. C. He smiled and said "Follow me." We followed him around to the back of the bus. He told us to say **OINK** 3 times as loudly as we could.

Dr. C lifted up his hat.

**There was the
Reading Pig!!**

I'm so happy Dr. C and the Reading
Pig came with us to the Desert
Wildlife Center. We had fun and
learned so much about the amazing
desert animals and plants!

I can't wait to go back!

# Match these desert animals to their names

- Javelina

- Roadrunner

- Prairie Dog

- Mountain Lion

- Big Horn Sheep

- Screech Owl

- Quail

CPSIA information can be obtained
at www.ICGtesting.com
Printed in the USA
BVHW060921010319
541487BV00001B/1